W9-CMZ-779

For A.M.B., who knows about beaches

THE
SMALL POTATOES'
BUSY BEACH DAY

Harriet Ziefert
Illustrated by Richard Brown

A Young Yearling

Published by
Dell Publishing
a division of
Bantam Doubleday Dell Publishing Group, Inc.
666 Fifth Avenue
New York, New York 10103

ISBN: 0-440-48045-0

Printed in the United States of America

August 1986

10   9   8   7   6

CW

CHAPTER ONE

TO THE BEACH

Hi. Meet the *Small Potatoes*.

They are a group of good friends.

They have a club and a clubhouse.

Right now, they're off to the beach!

Everybody is carrying something.

Even Spot, Molly's dog.

He has a beach towel.

So does Sue.

Scott has a hobo bag.

Molly has a rubber tube.

Chris and Sam are both carrying

the picnic basket.

And it looks heavy!

Roger has a kite and a Frisbee.

But—

Who has the beach ball?

And the beach blanket?

And the suntan oil?

The gang trooped toward the water.

Past the sunbathers.

Past little kids hunting for shells
in the wet sand.

Molly chased her rubber tube and ran ahead
of the rest.
At a good dry spot she shouted, "Let's put
    our stuff here!"

Guess what?

There was no beach blanket.

But the towel Spot had carried was pretty big.

Molly spread it on the sand.

They all put their sneakers on the edges

to keep the towel from blowing away.

"What's in your bag?" Sue asked Scott.

Scott put his hobo bag on the towel.

He untied it slowly.

"You have suntan oil!" Molly said.

"And a beach ball we can blow up!" Sam said.

"What's that?" asked Chris, pointing to
a small plastic case.

Scott answered, "Those are my earplugs.
Made to fit my ears. I have tubes in my ears,
so I'm not allowed to get water in them."

"Tubes?" asked Chris. "What kind of tubes?"

"Little plastic ones," answered Scott. "The
ear doctor put them in so I wouldn't get
so many ear infections."

"Do the tubes hurt?"

"No, they don't hurt if I keep my ears dry,"
said Scott. "But if I get water in my ears,
it feels terrible."

"I hope I never need ear tubes," said Molly.

"Me neither," said Sue.

Spot barked.

Something noisy was overhead.

It was a small airplane flying low
along the shoreline.

Trailing behind it was a sign:

HOT DOGS AND COLD SODA

AT HARRY'S BEACH BARN

"I'm hungry!" Chris said after he read the sign.

"Me too!" Sam said

"*Arf! Arf!*" barked Spot.

"But we just got here!" said Roger.

"Let's do something before we eat," said Sue.

"But what should we do?"

"We can hunt for shells," Sue answered.

"Good idea!" said Molly. "I'd rather play first
        and eat later."

Roger, Sue, and Scott agreed.

And Chris and Sam grumbled, "Okay."

But not Spot.

He stood next to the picnic basket,

panting and whining.

"Come over here," called Molly,

        feeling sorry for Spot.

Then she threw a stick in the air.

Molly knew a game of throw-and-catch

would take Spot's mind off lunch.

Everybody headed down the beach
to look for shells.

Even Spot.

But he kept looking back toward the beach towel.

He wanted to make sure no one
touched the food while he was gone.

Don't worry, Spot!

It will be there when you get back.

CHAPTER TWO

SEASHELLS BY THE SEASHORE

Roger found the first good shell.

It wasn't broken.

The halves were still attached.

Roger peeked inside, but it was empty.

Someone knew it was a mussel shell—because of the dark blue color and the long, oval shape.

"I found a clam shell with a hole in it!"
  shouted Sue.

"I wonder what made the hole," said Scott.

"Not a drill!" Chris said.

"And not the clam!" added Sue.

"Maybe it was a fish trying to get inside the clam
  to eat it," suggested Scott.

"That makes sense," said Chris. "If people like the
  insides of clams, I guess fish could too."

"Yuk!" said Sue, as she thought of a fish
  sucking out the juicy insides of a clam.

Sam found a crab.

It had bits of seaweed on its back.

The shell was creepy-looking.

And pretty disgusting.

Sam knew he could have some fun with it.

He took the crab and brushed it against Molly's leg.

Molly jumped.

"Ouch!" she screamed. "There's something
    biting me!"

Sam laughed.

But Molly didn't think the joke was funny.

Neither did Spot.

He growled at Sam.

"What's this?" asked Scott, holding up something
    with a shell like a helmet and a mouth
    like a swordfish.

"It's weird," said Roger.

"And ugly!" added Sam.

But no one knew its name.

So Scott decided to ask the lifeguard.

Scott headed for the lifeguard stand, holding
the shell in the air as he ran.

Scott and the lifeguard talked.

Soon Scott ran back, shouting as he came, "It's a
crab! A horseshoe crab! And it shuffles
along the sea bottom leaving a trail
in the sand."

By now everyone had something:
a clam, a mussel, or a scallop shell;
a crab, a snail, or a starfish.
They were all pretty easy to find—at least
Sue thought so.
She wanted something different.
Something pretty—like a sea horse.
A sea horse is small.
Only a few inches long.
And delicate.
Its face looks like a horse.
And Sue loved horses.
Sue wanted a sea horse a lot.
She wanted to take one home and put it
on her shelf.
But there wasn't one to be seen.
At least, not yet.

"What's the biggest fish in the sea?"
Chris asked Roger.

"A whale!" answered Roger immediately.

"Wrong!" said Chris.

"I'm not wrong!" argued Roger. "You're stupid!"

"I'm not stupid!" yelled Chris. "You're the stupid one! The biggest fish in the sea is the great white shark."

"But whales are bigger!"

"But whales are not fish, dummy! They're mammals! And I didn't ask about the biggest animal in the sea, did I?"

Molly heard the argument.

"Quit it!" she said. "Why don't we do something else?"

"What?" Sam asked.

"I think we should walk back to our towel
and put our shells away.
Then let's go swimming."
"I agree," said Sue.
So did everyone else—even Chris and Roger.
It was getting hot, and a quick swim
before lunch seemed like a good idea.

CHAPTER THREE

THE WATER'S COLD

Scott got his earplugs.

Molly got her rubber tube.

Everyone walked to the water's edge—at

a place where the lifeguard could see them.

The swimming area was roped off with
bright yellow buoys.

Sue was brave.

She rushed into the water and dived in.

"How could you do that?" Molly asked.
"The water's so cold!"

"If you get wet fast, it doesn't seem so cold,"
Sue answered.

Molly took Sue's advice.

She dunked fast, then climbed into her tube.

Molly looked comfortable with her arms
and legs drooping off the sides.

Drifting slowly away from shore, she looked
like a big fish sleeping in the sun.

Neither Chris nor Sam would get himself wet.

So they splashed each other.

And Spot too.

Scott waded in up to his waist.

And Roger didn't want to get wet at all.

"Come on in!" Sue shouted. "The water's nice!"

But Roger didn't want to swim.

"I'd rather watch," he answered.

Then he sat down on the beach.

Roger dug his toes into the sand and hoped
no one would bother him.

He didn't really like the ocean.

"There are things in there," he said to himself.

"Live animals. I don't want to swim with them."

Roger was scared and he hoped no one
would notice.

Spot began to bark.

Molly had drifted out pretty far and he wanted her to come back.

Molly heard Spot's bark and started
to paddle toward the beach.

Sue hitched a ride when Molly paddled by.

Sue helped by kicking with both feet while
Molly paddled with her hands.

Chris, Sam, and Scott played in the waves.
Chris was good at jumping the waves and
riding them in to shore.
A big wave dunked Sam, but he got up laughing.
'I got salt water up my nose,'' he said, snorting.
But he didn't seem to mind.
Scott caught a runaway raft and took a quick
ride before someone said, ''It's mine!''

Roger watched his friends.

And he watched the waves.

He imagined the waves were hungry animals.

Animals who roared.

Animals who showed their teeth in rows of whit

and opened up their jaws to bite.

Scott interrupted Roger's daydreaming.

"Look at my pruney fingers," he said,

shoving them in front of Roger's nose.

"They're disgusting," said Roger.

"No, they're not," said Scott. "It's from the water.

And the wrinkles will go away soon."

"Well, I'm glad my fingers don't look like prunes,"

said Roger.

Molly and Sue came out of the water.

Sam and Chris did too.

"Race you to the towel," yelled Sam.

It looked like everyone was in a big rush
for lunch. Especially Spot.

CHAPTER FOUR

SAND CASTLES

Chris opened the picnic basket.

He gave out the sandwiches and the drinks.

"Are there any chips?" asked Sam.

"There's one big bag for everyone," Chris answered.

He put it in the middle.

Everyone grabbed a handful.

Lunch didn't last long.

Sue and Scott, Molly and Sam, Roger, Chris—

all of them were fast eaters.

And Spot?

He ate the leftover bread crusts.

He even licked the salty crumbs from

the bottom of the potato chip bag.

Then Molly gave him two dog biscuits.

"What's for dessert?" Sue asked.

Chris pulled a bag of fruit from the
picnic basket.

"Peach or plum?" he asked.

Everyone picked a favorite fruit.

"Mine's so juicy!" said Sue.

"Mine too," said Scott. "It's dribbling down my
stomach and into my belly button!"

"And my hands are sticky," added Sam.

"So wash them in the ocean," said Chris.

"No, that's not a good idea," said Roger.
"The water's too salty. But it's fresh
at the showers."

"Who'll come with me?" asked Sam.

Everyone wanted to go.

So the gang trooped up the beach to the
shower stalls.

On the way they stopped to throw the garbage
into a trash can.

"What should we do now?" Sam asked.

"Let's build a castle," said Molly.

"And dig a moat around it," added Roger.

"*Arf! Arf!*" said Spot, kicking the sand
with his paws.

Roger and Sue worked on the castle.
Molly went looking for Popsicle sticks.
She knew they could be used as flags.
Sam borrowed a big pail and filled it
with water again and again.

Chris dug the moat.

Spot helped him dig it.

They worked for a long time.

All of them were very busy.

"This is the best sand castle I ever made,"
Roger said.

"And the biggest!" added Molly.

Sam noticed that the tide was coming in.

He was glad, because he was getting tired
of carrying pails of water.

The water's coming very close," he yelled.

Suddenly, one big spill filled the moat.

Sam smiled, happy that the walls were big
and strong enough to hold the water.

Roger said, ''The ocean's filled our moat
with junk!''

''Like seaweed.''

And sticks.''

And a sea horse.''

That's not junk!'' shouted Sue. ''Let me
have it! Please!''

Sue held the sea horse carefully.

She smiled and said, ''This is just what I wanted.''

There are starfish, snails, clams, mussels, and crabs in the ocean.

There are squid and jellyfish.

And octopuses.

And many, many other animals.

Thousands of different kinds.

But Sue thought she had the prettiest of all.

She was really happy.

So happy.

CHAPTER FIVE

GO FLY A KITE

What should we do now? Our sand castle is gone!''
moaned Chris.

''Too bad,'' said Molly. ''It was so nice.''

Everybody knew sand castles didn't last.

But it was sad when big waves wrecked them.

"I want to sunbathe," Molly said.

"I want to play Frisbee," said Roger.

Scott said, "I'd rather play ball."

"Bow-wow!" barked Spot.

"You see," said Scott, "he wants to play too."

"But we don't all have to do the same thing
said Molly.

Right!

"Roger, can I use the kite?" asked Chris.

"Can I share it?" asked Sam.

"Yes," said Roger to both of them.

So Sam and Chris went to find a good spot
for kite-flying.

Molly got comfortable.

Scott started to blow up the beach ball.

Roger threw the Frisbee to Spot.

And Spot made a good catch.

Sam made sure the cross-sticks were
in the right places.
Chris said, "Check the string too."
Sam looked and said it was all right.
It was pretty windy, and getting even windier.
Chris thought flying the kite would be easy.
He ran down the beach holding the kite
behind him.
He hoped it would lift off.
But it only dragged on the ground.
Sam said, "Let me try."
"No," said Chris, "I want to try again."
Chris tried and tried to get the kite into the air.
But he couldn't seem to do it.
"Dumb kite," he muttered.
The kite just wouldn't sail.
Chris felt like breaking it to bits.
But he knew that wouldn't help anything.
He yelled, "I'm mad. Really mad. Too mad
        to fly a kite. So you try."
He tossed the kite in Sam's direction.

The wind was really gusty.

Sam was lucky.

The kite took off with his first run.

It sailed above the boys' heads.

It dipped and dived and snapped its tail.

It soared.

It climbed.

And then—

When the wind rested, it fell.

"Roll the string back," shouted Chris.

"I'm doing it," said Sam, as he ran with the kite.

But he couldn't run fast enough.

The kite came back to earth.

CRASH!

Chris and Sam hurried toward the fallen kite.

"Anything break?" asked Sam, as he watched
Chris inspect the kite.

"Looks okay," said Chris. "Now I'm going
to try to fly it."

"Just take it easy and don't get mad," said Sam.
"Get a good grip, then run fast."

Chris gripped the string.

He ran into the wind.

And pretty soon the kite was flying high.

"Let out some more string!" shouted Sam.

"I'm going to try a loop-the-loop," Chris
shouted back.

"Don't get fancy," said Sam, "or you'll be sorry."

"You're right," said Chris. "I'll just
pull it in slowly."

Molly was alone on the towel.

She closed her eyes and listened to the waves beating on the shore.

She listened to the gulls squawking.

They're probably fighting over a piece of food, she thought.

She listened to Roger, Spot, and Scott playing ball.

But she didn't want to join them.

She felt like being alone.

Just wiggling her toes in the air and digging her heels in the sand.

Doing nothing but catching the sun.

Putt-putt-putt!

The noise of a plane made Molly sit up.

She put her hands over her eyes and squinted into the sun.

SUN WITH TIGER-TAN! said the banner flying from the plane.

Ooops!

Molly remembered she had forgotten to put on suntan oil.

She hoped it wasn't too late.

A sunburn hurts.

And tingles.

And itches.

And peels.

"I'd better go ask Scott if I can use his oil," said Molly.

And off she ran.

"Scott, I need suntan oil. Can I use yours?"
Molly shouted.

"Yeah."

Molly saw that Scott was busy playing and didn't feel like having a conversation.
Spot didn't pay any attention to her either.
So Molly turned and left.

Back at the towel Molly rubbed on the oil.

Then she sat down, cross-legged.

She noticed that her foot bottoms were

spotted with black.

She tried to rub the black spots off, but couldn't.

The stuff was sticky, not like ordinary dirt.

Molly realized it must be tar.

Yucky beach tar.

Too bad ships pollute the ocean with this gook,

she thought.

Too bad.

When Molly lay back on the towel, something
wet plopped between her eyes.

At first she thought it was from a big bird.

Then Molly realized it was starting to rain.

Drip Drip Drip

Plop!

By the time Molly stood up, everyone was
running toward her.

CHAPTER SIX

IT'S WET

It's raining!'' Sam cried.

So what,'' said Molly. ''We're wet already.

And the rain feels good on my fried skin!''

But everyone else is packing up.''

"We don't have to do what everyone else does,
    said Molly.

"Yeah."

"We can stay here and still have fun," said Chris

"What can we do?"

"We can do a rain dance," said Molly.

    She stood on top of a big rock.

    She stretched her arms.

    She threw back her head.

    The warm raindrops fell on Molly.

    Rain trickled down her nose and chin.

    Her arms and legs became wet and shiny.

"I'm a rainy thing now," she said.

    Then she shouted, "Come on, everybody.

        Let's dance."

Chris began the dance.

Then Sam and Scott joined in.

And finally Roger and Sue.

Spot stood in the middle and howled.

"This is fun," said Scott.

"I feel clean," said Roger.

"Me too," said Scott. "Cleaner than if I'd tak
a zillion baths."

"I feel like shouting," said Sam. "Shouting
the fish . . . and the birds . . ."

"So why don't you," said Molly. "There's
no one else on the beach."

"FISH—FISH IN THE SEA—DO YOU HEAR M
DO YOU HEAR THE RAIN?" Sam shoute

The fish didn't answer.

But the rain did, by making soft splashing
sounds as the drops fell on the water.

"It's starting to rain pretty hard now," said Roge

"Harder than a drizzle."

"I think we'd better go," said Sue.

"Before it pours."

Everybody agreed.

So they gathered up their stuff.

The tube.

The picnic basket.

The kite and the Frisbee.

Scott threw his hobo bag over his shoulder.

"Don't forget the towel," he reminded Molly.

The gang trooped away from the water.

Past the lifeguard stand.

Past the full trash baskets.

Good-bye, fish.

Good-bye, ocean.

Good-bye, lifeguard.

Good-bye, beach.

It's been a busy beach day for the *Small Potatoe.*

See ya at the next meeting!

SMALL POTATOES FUN

- Learn something new about shells, then teach what you learned to a friend.

- Since you now are a member of the *Small Potatoes Club*, make a membership card for yourself. You can copy the one below or invent your own.